THREE
SPOOKY
STORIES

THREE SPOOKY STORIES

Tom Leveen

Three Spooky Stories

Tom Leveen

Hello, my friend! Here for your entertainment are three "spooky" short stories, and I use sarcastic quotes there because of the three, only one is even a tiny bit spooky; the other two are supposed to be on the funny side of spooky. Here's hoping they are.

You may have seen these pieces performed live at Is What Is Is Theatre, Chyro Arts Venue, Changing Hands Bookstore, or Poisoned Pen Bookstore, in which case, I hope you remember them fondly.

Take a break, enjoy, smile. And of course . . . Happy Halloween.

~ Tom

Killer-Con

The agenda for the convention looked promising. Mike was anxious for it to start, and he squirmed impatiently while in line for his name tag.

8 am – Coffee and continental breakfast hosted by Starbucks.

9 am – Walking vs. Running: How to catch sprinting co-eds while moving at a brisk walk through thick foliage.

12 pm – Lunch. Cannibal-friendly.

1 pm – Machete or Axe? How Weapon Choice Affects Performance

4 pm – Dinner

6 pm – We Don't Need No Stinkin' Chainsaws: How Moving Parts Can Ruin a Good Massacre

8 pm – Film Festival. Hollywood's laugh-out-loud take on the profession, and how they get it all wrong. Complimentary popcorn and soft drinks! Cash bar available.

Grinning to himself, Mike turned over the flyer to see the following day's activities. Like any convention, attendance would be low Sunday morning, but the Con was thorough, cramming as much information into the weekend as possible. Mike figured he'd at least pick up the presentations that began after lunch.

11 am – To Mask or Not To Mask? How concealing your identity works for and against your victims.

12 pm – Luncheon and networking. Poolside! Visit our exhibition booths for free blade sharpening, with skin-crafts for the kids!

2 pm – Racism and Sexism in the Profession: Why always pick on the minority in the group? Plus, why sexually active teens must perish in fountains of their own arterial blood.

4 pm – Awards Ceremony

Mike's black, merciless heart gave a little jump. The awards ceremony! He dared to imagine his bloodstained fingers grasping the KillerCon Best Member Award this year. That damned sociopath Jay had cheated him out of it three years running, and it was time the organizers of the event realized Mike's talent. Didn't mutilations count for anything anymore? What about unique use of weaponry? Jay was a hack-and-slash man all the way, had been since birth, but Mike had never limited himself to a solitary weapon—weapons of opportunity were his stock in trade, from butcher knives to hacksaws.

Plus, Jay always wore that stupid clown mask all the time, even during the convention. It was permitted, but frowned upon. How come, Mike wondered, when every other serial killer and mass murderer was willing to show his face, Jay was rewarded for covering his own?

Mike dropped the convention program and flyers back into the bloody canvas tote the Con had provided for all the attendees. He glanced down into the bag, still waiting in line to receive his nametag. This year's swag wasn't as outstanding as last year's, he noted with some disdain. A sharpening stone (so trite), a knife-shaped letter opener (cliché), and brand-new work gloves for the more down-and-dirty work their trade required.

Mike rolled his eyes. If he didn't win Best Member this year, he determined, then this was his last Con for awhile. So what if they cancelled his membership? It wasn't a union; his work would go on unimpeded. And, he further determined as his mind wandered on the gory subject, he'd make this year his most fatal yet. Twenty co-eds? Heck with that, he was going for a whole dorm full of them! Let's see Jay keep up with that kind of body count at a stupid summer camp!

Mike grunted as someone bumped into him from behind. He turned slowly, letting his bloodshot eyes narrow into crimson slits.

It was Jay. Mike recognized the dopey clown mask instantly.

"Hello, Jay," Mike said, sneering.

The clown mask bobbled. "Mike," Jay replied.

Mike continued to peer through the mask's eyeholes, burning his hatred into the other killer. "You gonna apologize or what?"

"For what?"

"You bumped into me!"

"Mike, you're being overly sensitive."

"Overly what!?" Mike exploded. "Why you third-rate, maim-only, sequel-bombing! . . ."

Jay's machete cut cleanly through Mike's neck, sending the other man's head toppling end over end past the line of convention attendees. There was a shocked gasp through the crowd--not at the grisly sight of Mike's lips fish-mouthing foamy cries of agony, but rather at the breach of etiquette. Killers didn't kill each other at the Con, that was the rule.

Jay stared emptily at the rest of the attendees in line, who turned away and waited for their nametags. No one wanted to cross a three-time Best Member award winner.

Jay wiped his machete off on Mike's grease and blood-stained coveralls, noting with detached delight that one foot was still twitching.

The rest of the convention passed uneventfully, and everyone went back to work Monday with a greater appreciation for their chosen career.

It was going to be a red-letter year.

Alone

I am lonely.

It's a tangible thing, more tangible than me. They see right through me, now as ever, only now, it's for real.

I've never been so alone in my entire life.

Wait.

That's not exactly true. I've never been so alone in general.

I've also never been so cold.

I wander the halls of my school, growing more and more angry that this is where I ended up. Of all places.

Sometimes I try to sleep, but the most I can manage is sort of a floating doze.

This sucks.

Monday is hard. School is packed full. I guess I don't get a holiday named after me. I drift from group to group, listening carefully. But I don't even hear my name mentioned.

Guess I shouldn't be surprised. I didn't exist then. I don't exist now.

When Jordon Kersey and her clan of pretentious troglodytes talk about my best friend Hallie, though, that's even worse. I swing at Jordan, because really, what's anyone going to do about it?

I don't connect. Of course. I am a ghost.

Her clan starts heading for the staircase leading down to the first floor, and I follow along, swinging, swinging, nothing happening, and it makes me even more mad.

Then, just as she's taking the first step, I scream as loud as I can and use both hands to push. The scream, of course, is composed of pure silence, an empty orchestra.

But my ghostly hands connect.

Jordon gasps and flies down the stairs. She lands once somewhere in the middle, bounces, and flies again before sliding to a stop on the linoleum floor.

Some people laugh. A few shout in surprise. Some applaud, like Jordon's committed the worst high school blunder ever.

She doesn't get up.

That's when the girls' coach crashes through the crowd that's gathered and checks for a pulse.

That's how I learn that I can kill. Not all at once, but by degrees. One by one.

I stalk through the halls each day, watching them go busybusy helterskelter to this class and that, did you hear what Ricky said to Sheila last night omigod! My ears burn and bleed at the sound they make, except my ears can no longer hear for they are not there.

Nights are easier. Quiet. There's an occasional hum that I learned came from the air conditioning units. I can thrust my incorporeal head into the workings and I've learned a lot about these machines. I would have been a fine air conditioning repairwoman.

Dude did you see the game last night, dude of course I did dude!

My parents are so totally lame I sweardagod did I tell you what they did yesterday?

Ohmigod I failed algebra my mom will kill me!

Not if I kill you first, I think. At least, I think I think. What do you think, I ask as if aloud, but it's silent and quiet, because my body has long since gone.

I want to leave the school but I don't. I am a superhero, I am X-Man Kitty Pryde. Walls are no longer barriers to me, but still I avoid the gym. They killed me there. With their mocking, their hate, their vitriol, ha ha ugly girl, can't get a date, can't go to parties, can't be cool like us.

I think (if I can think) there was something wrong from the beginning, from before I was born perhaps, some defect or misalignment of my heart that made it give up the ghost, ha ha, at the age of fifteen. Panic struck me daily, taxing the organ, boiling my blood and twisting my guts like snakes in burlap, until that day during gym class when it became too much and my heart said "See ya!" and lay down and slept. I watched, invisible and go-through-able, as they kept on with their jokes, made fun of my body until someone finally realized this was no game, no show, no fake, that I was dead and gone, then hushed ripples of disbelief echoed around the gym. I watched it all, floating above them.

I wonder (if I can wonder) what my father did with my body. I think I can leave the school, I think I could go and see, but I don't. I stay and watch because I do not sleep now, and I test the limits of my disembodied strength, and finally learn that I can kill.

I tried Jeff a week after Jordan, exerting my will on him and throttling his veins until an embolism shocked his brain to death.

I hear them talking these days about the school being haunted. That some thing is watching and choosing and waiting and striking.

They are right.

But I am still alone.

I have not seen Jordan or Jeff. They are not bound here like me, it seems. I wonder why. Or maybe they are here, but even I cannot see them. That's not what the movies would have me believe. I haven't seen a movie in a long time.

I watch my best friend Hallie closely. I pretend I am her guardian angel, and perhaps I am. They have always attacked her as they did me, but her heart is strong, she will not perish like I did, panic and fear choking the drumbeat in her chest to stillness. She is sad that I am gone, so I am sad for her. I never meant to leave her. But I follow her every day, watch her in class, try to whisper answers in her ear that I don't think she can hear.

So when she choked on a piece of meat at lunch yesterday, my heart (if I had one) was torn apart. I watched my best friend die. It was long and painful, not the brief spasm I had felt. I screamed and no one heard. I wept and no one could dry the imaginary tears.

But I heard laughter. Laughter that wasn't from a living thing. I heard laughter and taunting, the sound of victory, the sound of a girl and a boy celebrating. I am a ghost, yet felt a chill.

I am not alone.

DINOSAURS DOWNSTAIRS

When Bill went downstairs to the street to start his car that morning, he was dismayed to see it had been crushed flat.

His baby, his darling 1966 Camero, cherry red, was now reduced to a foot-high mass of rectangular metal. The other cars lined up on the street were untouched. Bill knew immediately is was his downstairs neighbor, the dinosaur.

They shouldn't let dinosaurs sub-let here, Bill thought angrily. There were plenty of apartments in the city, why on earth did the management feel it was imperative to allow an extinct species to live here next to so many humans?

Plus they were dangerous. Sure, the Tyrannosaurus Rex downstairs had sworn up and down that he was reformed, that he'd converted to a heart-healthy vegan diet, but Bill wasn't convinced. The ripping and tearing sounds he'd heard coming from beneath his apartment suggested a feast of meat, not dainty baby corn and bean sprouts. Bill had complained to the manager, who'd only shrugged and said the Rex paid his rent on the dot every month, so it wasn't any of his concern what went on in the privacy of the dinosaur's apartment.

The manager had, no doubt, informed the Rex of Bill's complaints. And that's why his Camero was now the height of a fire hydrant.

"Fricking dinosaurs!" Bill turned on his heel to go back into the building. Will insurance even cover this? he wondered as he banged into the building.

We won, they lost! he thought as he stomped up the stairs to the second floor. "Dinosaurs had their shot, and nature selected them for extinction," was a line from some dinosaur movie he'd seen once, and those words delighted him endlessly. It was a mammal's world now, Bill told himself, and dinosaurs had no business taking homes and jobs away from decent, hard-working, tax-paying citizens like himself. They flooded the health care system, took resources away from the schools--nothing good ever came from a dinosaur! Well . . . maybe oil, but that was eons ago.

Bill worked himself up into a rage by the time he reached the Rex's apartment on the second floor. He pounded angrily on it.

"I know you're in there! I can hear you stomping around! Come out here! I want to know what you did to my car!"

Bill was surprised when a brachiosaur opened the apartment door. He almost couldn't see the tiny head perched atop her long neck.

"Oh! I--I'm sorry, I--I'm looking for the tyrannosaur."

"He's not here," the brach said stiffly.

"Oh . . . Well, you tell him from me that I know he's the one who crushed my Camero out there, and he's going to have to pay for it. Every last cent! You got that?"

The brachiosaur nodded. "I'll let him know."

Bill was suddenly sure that the brach had no intention of reporting his complaint. His anger blossomed fully, and he aimed to take it out on the plant-eater.

"Fucking herbivores! Now you look here! I don't care how few of you there are left in the world, but you can't just barge into my town and start crashing around like you own the place! We're the dominant species, see? This is our world now, and you don't belong here. Why don't you just go back to where you came from? Fucking dinos! If it was up to me, I'd send every last rotten one of you back to your--"

The brachiosaur stepped on Bill. His skeletal system collapsed instantly, and he was reduced to a crimson stain about the thickness of a manhole cover. Ironically, he could likely fit into the Camero now.

"Honey?" the Rex called from the bathroom. "What's going on? Did you feel the floor shake just now?"

The brachiosaur wiped her foot on the welcome mat, and shut the door easily with one faint brush of her tail. The Rex poked his head out of the bathroom, trying to floss several pounds of cabbage and onions out from between his razor teeth with a length of nylon rope. His weak forelegs weren't up to the task, and vegetation clung stubbornly to his gums.

The brachiosaur turned to him, smiling sweetly. "Nothing to worry about. It was just a mammal."

Tom Leveen is a Bram Stoker Award finalist and an award-winning novelist, who has also written for the comic book series *Spawn*. For free books and more information, please check out

linktr.ee/tomleveen

If you enjoyed this short book, please consider leaving a review! Thank you!